SCRIBBLY

Ged Adamson

HARPER
An Imprint of HarperCollinsPublishers

ISBN 978-0-06-267082-3

The artist used pencil and watercolor paints
to create the illustrations for this book.
Typography by Jeanne Hogle
21 22 23 24 25 RTLO 10 9 8 7 6 5 4 3 2 1
❖
First Edition

FOR imaginary friends
and dogs everywhere

Last summer, Mom and I
moved to a new town.
It was kind of exciting!

There was a bunch of
fun stuff to do

and lots of cool things to see.

Everything was so big and amazing!
But there was something missing
from our new home—

someone to play with.

"If only I had a friend," I thought, "everything would feel just right." That gave me an idea.

I sat down and
I began to draw.

I used a lot of paper.

I even added flowers.

It just needed a finishing touch.

Something special . . .

"At last!

A masterpiece."

I called him Scribbly because he was kind of . . . scribbly.
But to me he was just right.

Scribbly was the bestest friend anyone could ask for.
He was always happy to play.

and sometimes he was a little naughty, too.
But I didn't mind.

Scribbly did everything a regular dog did,
and that made me happy.

My mom tried to help out with Scribbly when she could,
but she thought I was too old for a pretend dog.

She didn't always find Scribbly as much fun as I did.

Still, I think Mom mostly liked that I was having a nice time.

Especially because it meant I was
totally beat before bed.

Then one day, Mom told me she had some great news.
"Louie from upstairs invited you to his birthday party."

I wasn't so sure that was great news.
It isn't always easy meeting new people.

"Maude, it might be a good idea to leave Scribbly at home," Mom said.

"Okay, Mom."

6TH FLOOR

I told her I would think about it.

When I arrived at Louie's party, I tried to have fun, but I felt nervous. The more kids arrived at the party, the more nervous I felt.

I really tried not to bring Scribbly.

But I really, really needed him.

Louie was curious about who I was talking to
and asked to be introduced.

"Don't be shy, Scribbly," I said.

Scribbly did a backflip . . .

and helped himself to some cake.

He didn't have any trouble making new friends.

In the end, everybody wanted to play with Scribbly.

He made being the new kid much easier.

When we got home, Scribbly was exhausted.
That's when Mom told me we should have a little talk.

"I'm proud of you. Going to a party where you don't know a lot of people can be hard, but you did a good job," Mom said.

"The other kids liked me . . . thanks to Scribbly."

My mom pulled me closer.

"They like you because of you.

You taught Scribbly how to dance,

how to draw,

and how to do magic.

Scribbly is special and fun because YOU ARE," she said.
I started to feel better, like things were going to be all right.

The next day, Mom said she had a surprise.
I asked her if I could bring Scribbly.

"Yes, absolutely. I think Scribbly will like this surprise," replied Mom.

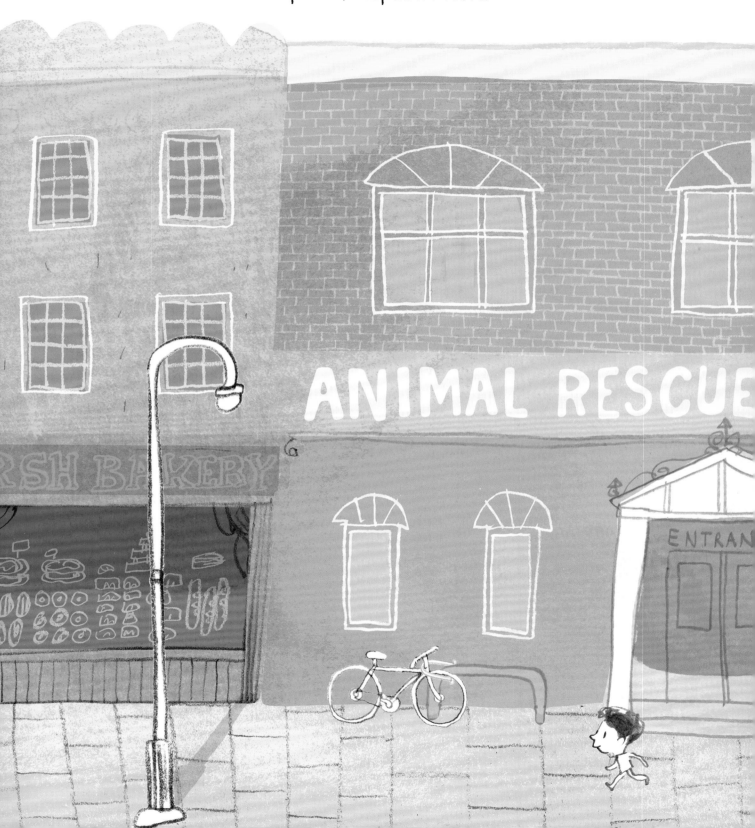

Mom was right. I never saw Scribbly so excited.

"Scribbly, look! We've got a new friend!"

And just like that, everything was more than just right.

Things were scribbnificent!